T0406976

FINDING HOME,

a Hawaiian Petrel's Journey

FINDING HOME,

a Hawaiian Petrel's Journey

CAREN LOEBEL-FRIED

UNIVERSITY OF
HAWAI'I PRESS
HONOLULU

Library of Congress Cataloging-in-Publication Data

Names: Loebel-Fried, Caren, author, illustrator.
Title: Finding home : a Hawaiian petrel's journey / Caren Loebel-Fried.
Description: Honolulu : University of Hawai'i Press, [2024] | Includes
    bibliographical references | Summary: Eleven-year-old Makani finds her
    own way to help her biologist mom save the beloved and endangered
    Hawaiian petrels. Includes facts about the Hawaiian petrels and their
    connection to Hawaiian culture and history
Identifiers: LCCN 2023056391 (print) | LCCN 202305 (ebook) | ISBN
    9780824895716 (hardback) | ISBN 9780824898137 (pdf)
Classification: LCC PZ7.1.L628 Fi 2024 (print) | LCC PZ7.1.L628 (ebook) |
    DDC [Fic]—dc23
LC record available at https://lccn.loc.gov/2023056391
LC ebook record available at https://lccn.loc.gov/2023056392

University of Hawai'i Press books are printed on acid-free
paper and meet the guidelines for permanence and
durability of the Council on Library Resources.

Designed by Mardee Melton

*Dedicated to the seabirds, who make my heart soar;
to Megan Dalton, who introduced me to the ʻuaʻu and
inspired me to write this story; and to Lily, with love—
welcome to the world!*

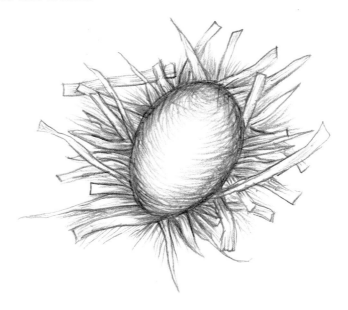

CONTENTS

FINDING HOME
The Story

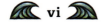

A HAWAIIAN PETREL'S JOURNEY
The Story behind the Story

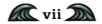

FINDING HOME

THE STORY

ʻUAʻU,
THE HAWAIIAN PETREL

Once upon a time, petrels filled the night skies of Hawaiʻi. During their nesting season, these seabirds flew in from the ocean at dusk, squeaking, barking, giggling, and growling, weaving great arcs in the sky. They chased each other in twos and threes, calling out their own name: "ʻUaʻu! [oo-WAH-oo!] ʻUaʻu!" There were so many petrels, they blackened the sky! And in deep, dark burrows underground, from the sea up to the mountaintops, their moans made the earth rumble.

Can you hear them?

Now, there are just a few burrows scattered high on the mountains of the Hawaiian Islands. Some burrows lie in loose orange soil under dense ferns, some are hidden inside moist rocky crevices, a handful are buried in gravelly hills of brown cinder, and here and there they are tucked inside cracks in old red *pāhoehoe* lava.

Where have the *ʻuaʻu* gone?

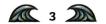

CHAPTER ONE

WHEN MAKANI WAS YOUNG

"Don't be sleepy, Makani!"

Makani Kealoha Morton grew up on the small Hawaiian island of Lānaʻi. Makani means "wind" in Hawaiian. Her parents named her after the air currents that seabirds depend upon. As a small child, Makani was quiet, thoughtful, and watchful. She loved running in the wind, and she adored seabirds.

On summer nights when she was little, her mom would sometimes say, "Let's *holoholo* to the colony!"

The colony!

Makani remembered those evenings . . .

Orange clouds painted the evening sky. Her dad drove their pickup truck with Makani up front, squeezed comfortably between her parents. She yawned, but felt her excitement rise as they rumbled and bounced up the rocky road. Makani leaned forward, squinting out the windshield, searching the darkening sky above them. But she couldn't see past the thick canopy of leaves overhead.

Her dad parked at the gate. Climbing up the steep path, Makani scrambled ahead of her parents. When small rocks made her slip, she steadied herself by grabbing the tough *uluhe* ferns growing alongside the trail. There was one place where the *uluhe* grew right across the path. Beneath the ferns, in the dim light, Makani spied a hole in the ground. It was the entrance to a burrow, an underground nest! Was there anyone inside? Makani strained to see or hear any activity.

Suddenly, she heard their calls from above . . .

"'Ua'u! 'Ua'u!"

"Come on, Makani!" her dad whispered, as her parents squeezed through a break in the *uluhe.* "Let's get up to the end of the trail before it's completely dark out!"

At the top of the path, Makani lay back on the springy *uluhe,* her mom and dad at her sides. She could feel the ground humming as the *'ua'u,* deep in their burrows, murmured to one another. Makani's body vibrated with the voices of the seabirds. She felt a rush of air on her face from an *'ua'u* flying low and close. She shivered with excitement and wonder.

Makani's dad handed her night-vision goggles. And then, the world of the *'ua'u* came to life before her eyes!

Dark silhouettes circled the moon and stars. On narrow wings, some outstretched, some bent, they flapped and glided. As the *'ua'u* sped by, their undersides flashed white, flipping to black as their dark topsides became a gleaming streak soaring in the other direction. Chasing one another, swooping, flapping, gliding, they called, "'Ua'u! 'Ua'u!"

Makani imagined having a petrel of her own, to make a burrow nest for, to feed and care for. She lowered the goggles and whispered, "Mom, can we bring a petrel chick home? Please?"

In the darkness, Makani could see her mom smile gently. "Makani, ʻuaʻu are not pets. They are wild creatures."

Makani opened her mouth, about to object, but then glanced up. She watched the seabirds sky-dancing in the darkness above. She heard their whispers and cries in the wind. She felt their murmurs in the ground beneath her. And then she understood. The ʻuaʻu *were* wild. And Makani loved their wildness.

Makani didn't know it then, but those nights on Lānaʻi with the ʻuaʻu would always be a part of her.

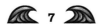

CHAPTER TWO

NIHOKŪ

Makani was older now, and her family lived on the northern tip of Kauaʻi.

Makani's mom, a seabird biologist, worked with the ʻuaʻu. In Hawaiʻi, ʻuaʻu chicks and adults were dying, even in the most hard-to-reach places. Something had to be done! But how could an island be made safe for nesting seabirds?

Makani's mom and her team had a plan.

They would create an "island within an island" at Nihokū in Kīlauea Point National Wildlife Refuge. A special fence that keeps out predators would be installed. Invasive plants and animals would be removed, and native plants planted. Nest boxes would be built and buried. They would transfer ʻuaʻu chicks from their burrows in the Nā Pali mountains to Nihokū, where the team would feed and care for the chicks. Hopefully, the chicks would imprint on Nihokū before they fledged and flew off to the sea. If the chicks remembered and trusted Nihokū, they might return there as adults, to this special place where they could raise their young in safety.

One day, while her mom was in the field preparing for the arrival of the chicks, Makani sat with her dad at their dining-room table. She asked him, "What does the name Nihokū mean, anyway?"

He said, "It's an old name. *Niho* means 'tooth' and *kū* means 'to stand, to rise.' The land looks just like that: a tooth sticking straight out!"

Makani grinned and laughed. Her dad continued.

"And while at sea, you can see this jutting-out piece of land when you approach it from any direction."

Makani nodded. Her dad smiled at her and said, "And there's even more. The foundation stones of a rock wall are also called *niho*. And *kū* means anchor."

"Wow! That's really cool." said Makani. "What a great name for a nesting colony." They both crossed their fingers and nodded to each other, smiling.

But then Makani's smile faded. Searching her dad's eyes, she said, "I feel bad for the chicks, and their parents. Why can't mom's team bring them all to Nihokū? Why separate them?"

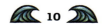

Her dad sighed. "Well, they can't bring the adult ʻuaʻu to Nihokū because they will just fly back to their mountain burrows, or out to the sea."

Makani looked down.

"A good thing to remember is this, Makani: next year, the adults will return to their natural burrows and try nesting again."

He paused, watching Makani as she frowned and rubbed at a stain on the table. He gathered her up in his arms.

"Hey, don't worry, my sweet girl. The chicks will be very well cared for at Nihokū. And, honestly, there's a good chance that they wouldn't have made it with their parents in the mountains . . . What's really sad to me is this: the ʻuaʻu and other seabirds were here for millions of years before we humans arrived. We've unintentionally made it very dangerous for them to nest in Hawaiʻi. It's possible that the ʻuaʻu will go extinct if we do nothing. We have to try to help them!"

Makani looked up at him, her eyes wide. He said, "You know, that's why Mom became a biologist."

Makani nodded. She wanted to help seabirds, too.

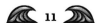

CHAPTER THREE

NESTING SEASON

ʻ*U*ʻ*au* live over the ocean, but they must come to land to raise their young. In the Nā Pali mountains of Kauaʻi, an ʻuaʻu couple had reunited in their burrow. It was the same place they had met the year before, and the year before that. And they would probably meet here again next year and the year after. Now, they cuddled and mated, then flew far out over the ocean to eat and build energy.

Over the sea, night and day, they sailed and soared, each to different places where they knew there was abundant food. All the while, a new life was developing inside the female ʻuaʻu.

Three weeks later, she returned alone to the Nā Pali mountains. Pinpointing their burrow and landing next to it, she scuttled inside and down the long, curving entrance. Deep inside, in a small cleared area, she sat at the center and arranged a few twigs and dried leaves around herself. She rocked and kicked. Then, while raising and lowering her tail, she widened her tail feathers and laid one gleaming white egg.

She inspected the egg carefully. It was perfect. She sat down to incubate, spreading herself out and wriggling her body until she completely covered the egg. The new life inside the egg needed warmth in order to live and grow.

Her mate returned to the burrow the next day, and she rose up, letting him settle down to incubate the egg. Thirsty and hungry, she left immediately, flying out to the sea to drink and eat.

Over the next fifty days, the couple took turns incubating their egg. One adult would come back with a full belly to relieve the brooding adult, who would then fly off for food and water. Neither parent would leave the egg until the other had returned. No matter if there were storms or high winds, they would always return to their burrow to share in the care of their egg.

Time to hatch! The chick worked all day to break free of her egg. Her father was there that day. He sometimes moved the egg slightly to a better position, but the chick had to do the rest. When she finally emerged from the egg, her downy feathers were wet, but they soon dried and fluffed out. She opened her eyes. The darkness of the burrow and the warmth of her father were a comfort to her in this new world.

A few days later, she could keep herself warm in her thick down coat. It was then that her parents left her alone in the burrow for the very first time. They both flew far away to gather food for her, bringing back nutritious fish oil to regurgitate into her hungry, insistent mouth. At first, they came to feed her frequently. But after a while, she would sometimes have to wait two weeks between meals. Even so, the chick grew and grew. She knew nothing of the dangers outside her burrow; she knew only hunger, warmth, fish oil, and the smell of the sea.

And soon, she would have a name.

CHAPTER FOUR

HAPE#4

Makani was dreaming. She was an ‘ua‘u, a Hawaiian petrel soaring over the ocean. When she woke up, she immediately thought of one ‘ua‘u chick she knew well.

It had been weeks since the first cohort of ‘ua‘u chicks were collected from their mountain burrows. When the helicopter arrived with the chicks, Makani had been there! The team members had carefully carried the five blue boxes from the helicopter to the van that would transport them to Nihokū. There were two chicks inside each box. Makani had imagined that the little fluffy chicks were frightened, and had sent them silent messages. "Don't be afraid! You're OK, little ones!"

Now, she threw back the sheet and yawned all the way down the hall to the kitchen. Her mom was grabbing lunch things from the refrigerator, filling water bottles, moving quickly.

Makani asked, "Are you going to feed the chicks?"

Her mom nodded, distracted. "Yup!"

"Can I come?"

Her mom looked at Makani and then quickly grabbed another water bottle. "*Ae!* But we have to hurry, Makani! Get dressed and grab something to eat. We need to *ʻāwīwī*, so be quick like the wind!"

"*ʻAʻole!* No, ʻIo! You can't go out!" Their cat meowed at the kitchen door as they were leaving. Of course, they had named him after a bird! ʻIo was a hunter, just like his namesake, the Hawaiian hawk. But ʻIo stayed inside the house, where he was safe from cars and diseases. And native birds were safe from him.

At the back entrance to the refuge, they climbed a winding path through the forest. The trees opened up to a grassy area. Makani could see the predator-exclusion fence snaking its way over hills and into valleys in both directions, all the way down to the ocean.

The team was already at the field station. For weeks, they had cared for the brood of ten Hawaiian petrel chicks. One sleepy chick at a time had been collected from its burrow box. Each chick had been weighed, had its wings measured, and fed just the right amount of fish slurry that had been warmed to just the right temperature. Their progress was recorded daily in a field notebook. Lately, almost every morning revealed another empty burrow box; a chick had fledged and flown to sea during the night!

Makani had learned that biologists give birds four-letter codes. Hawaiian petrels are called HAPE: "HA" from "Hawaiian," and "PE" from "petrel." HAPE#4 was one of the last chicks left from this first-year cohort at Nihokū.

Bobby, the lead biologist, gently held HAPE#4. He shook his head.

"Too sleepy to bite me, eh? Time for you to go and find your own breakfast!"

Her overall size was small. But her weight was good, and her wing coordinates were just right for her body size. It was time for HAPE#4 to fledge.

CHAPTER FIVE

CALL OF THE SEA

That night, the ʻuaʻu called HAPE#4 perched on a lava ridge above the ocean. She swayed slightly in the wind. A few fluffy down feathers blew in the breeze, but her sleek adult feathers stayed close to her body. Her legs and webbed feet were pink, but her toes looked like they had been dipped in black ink. Bright stars twinkled in the dark sky. Droplets of salty water clung to her wings, her chest, and her face.

She had wandered up through the tunnel before, drawn to the smells and sounds of the ocean. She had stretched out her long, thin wings and flapped vigorously. She had even felt a slight lift! And every time, she had turned and scurried back into her cozy, familiar burrow, just as she did tonight. But before she disappeared into darkness, the moon glinted on a tiny silver band she wore on her pink ankle.

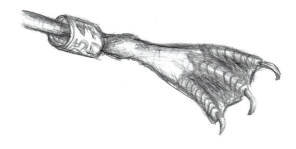

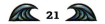

CHAPTER SIX

A GRAPH TELLS PART OF THE STORY

The next day, the sun sparkled on the silver bracelet Makani wore on her wrist, a gift from her parents for her eleventh birthday that year. Engraved onto the metal band was a swirling design, and winding through the lines of the design were the words "Makani—Wind."

The wind was blowing hard at Nihokū. Makani found Bobby behind the shed under the dancing trees. He was sitting on a ridge above the artificial burrows. Makani liked Bobby. He was smart and funny. She sat down next to him.

Bobby stared at a tablet, studying a graph that showed the growth of the translocated Hawaiian petrel chicks. Each chick had a uniquely colored line that moved on the graph according to their weight and wing measurements. The lines moved differently as they followed each chick's progress, but all of the lines moved upward; the chicks were growing well. When a chick fledged, its line stopped. Just a few lines continued, including the pink line that belonged to HAPE#4.

Makani waited quietly, staring at Bobby. She coughed, but he didn't look up. Finally, she said, "Do you think HAPE#4 will ever fledge?"

Bobby looked at her sharply. "Hush! I'm sciencing!"

Makani giggled. Bobby raised one eyebrow and scowled at her, pretending to be annoyed. Then he gave her a small smile before focusing again on his tablet. Through puckered lips, he let out a slow loud breath of air and said, "I don't know why HAPE#4 hasn't fledged."

He looked sideways at Makani. "Maybe she just wants to stick around and tear a little more flesh from my fingers."

Makani looked at the scars on his arms and hands. Those bites must have hurt! But she knew that Bobby loved these birds that he cared for so well.

"Truly, HAPE#4 seems fine in every way," he said, pointing to the pink line on the graph. "Maybe she'll head out tonight!"

The row of burrow boxes below them made a jagged line down the hill. Makani gazed down at them, thinking about the little bird that was fast asleep inside one of those boxes. Makani looked out at the ocean, wondering . . . Was HAPE#4 afraid to fly out to sea alone? If she did fledge, would she be able to find food on her own? But mostly, if HAPE#4 finally fledged, Makani worried, would she ever return to Nihokū?

CHAPTER SEVEN

HELP FOR A CHICK ON LĀNAʻI

"Makani," said her mom that afternoon, "an adult ʻuaʻu was found dead outside an active burrow on Lānaʻi. The nest camera showed it was killed by a cat."

"Oh no!" cried Makani.

"ʻAe," her mom nodded. "It takes two adults to raise one chick. Since it will be a little while before this chick fledges, Aunty Rae and her team are giving the chick supplemental feedings."

Rae and Tom were biologists, and her parents' closest friends. They were like family.

"We are going to Lānaʻi tomorrow, you, me, and Dad, to help Aunty Rae and Uncle Tom feed the chick."

Makani immediately started thinking. She asked, "How will we know how much fish slurry to feed the chick?"

Her mom brushed the hair from Makani's eyes and nodded, smiling with encouragement. "Great question. We're going to use data from our translocation project!"

"Wow! Perfect!" cried Makani.

"And our Big Island friends at the wildlife center are supplying the fish slurry and the permits. We are a great team working together to get this chick fledged!"

Makani smiled to herself. She was thrilled to be part of this team.

Tom picked them up at the small Lānaʻi airport. On the drive to Tom and Rae's house, Makani looked with pleasure at all the familiar sights. They paused in front of the sanctuary for feral cats, where Makani's family had adopted their pet cat, ʻIo. Makani chuckled at all the different cats, some climbing, others lounging, and many chasing each other and playing all over the well-equipped outdoor area. A big fence kept the cats safe from the dangers outside, and the nesting seabirds safe from the cats.

Tom shook his head. "There are loads of feral cats still roaming all over the mountains, but the sanctuary is at full capacity. There's no room for more cats."

At the house, Makani helped Rae pack a scale, a wing ruler, a cooler holding a syringe loaded with fish slurry, and a thermos of hot water to warm up the slurry. When they arrived at the burrow, the wildlife camera set up next to the entrance showed that no parent had come to deliver

a meal the night before. So, Makani's mom carefully pulled out the sleepy petrel chick. The chick woke suddenly and squirmed wildly, trying to break free. Makani's mom held the chick firmly while Rae did an examination. Tom wrote down the chick's weight, wing measurements, and other notes in a field notebook.

"She looks good," said Rae. "Her belly is empty, though."

Rae spoke quietly to the 'ua'u chick. "Here come some good eats, Little One!"

As Rae fed the chick warm fish slurry, Makani's dad took photos, and Makani documented everything in her field journal.

Driving back along the ridge, they stopped to look at a clearing where a predator-exclusion fence was being installed. Rae pointed to a dark green area across the valley.

"See the strawberry guava? In only ten years, these invasive plants have taken over big areas where *uluhe* ferns used to grow. *'Ua'u* like to dig their burrows in the soft soil under *uluhe*. Strawberry guava makes the soil too hard and packed for an *'ua'u* to dig out a burrow." Shaking her head, Rae said, "*'Ua'u* used to nest there, but not anymore."

From the back seat of the truck, sitting between her parents, Makani scanned the deep, black ridges carved into the side of the mountain. She remembered a long time ago her mom had said, "If anything ever happens to your dad and me, Aunty Rae and Uncle Tom will take good care of you." Makani wondered . . . Were there other orphaned, hungry chicks out there waiting in burrows, alone in the dark? Would there be anyone to help them?

Makani shivered. She reached for each of her parents' hands and held them tightly.

CHAPTER EIGHT

FORAGING FOR A LITTLE ONE

The next night, when they were back home, wind howled through the ironwood trees. Makani opened her bedroom window wide. She felt the energy of the storm. ʻIo lay next to her in bed, all warm, soft, and cuddly. A misty spray blew in. ʻIo looked out the window, then up at Makani, who absently patted him. ʻIo purred loudly and kneaded her arm, his sharp claws pressing in just enough to let Makani know he was there. But Makani was imagining a distant sea with a petrel flying over it, gathering food for her hungry chick, who waited in a burrow on Lānaʻi.

A thousand miles away, an ʻuaʻu soared. She followed a wind path northwest up the chain of the Hawaiian Islands. Around the islets and atolls of Papahānaumokuākea she flew, heading north toward the Aleutian Islands, then east past Alaska, and down off the coast of North America. At night, upwellings brought bioluminescent squid, lanternfish, and other small fish up from the dark ocean depths. Their sparkling blue lights and scent attracted the ʻuaʻu. Dashing across the ocean's

surface, she dipped her sharp hooked beak into the water, snatching and swallowing many small squid and fish.

She swooped, wheeled, arced, and glided, her flight relaxed and easy. The wind propelled her. She even slept while flying, half her brain awake while the other half rested. Her wings, thin and strong, cut through the air.

She flew and ate, all the while making a nutritious oil in her stomach for her chick. Finally circling back toward the chain of the Hawaiian Islands, she made a last dip for fresh fish. This would provide her chick with water.

She launched again with the help of the trade winds. The smells and stars guided her. And a map she could see and feel inside her pulled her like a magnet back to Lānaʻi, to her burrow, with a belly full of food for her hungry chick.

CHAPTER NINE

THE DARK SKY

Late the next evening, Makani and her dad stood on the deck outside their house. Makani gazed with concern at the bright lights from the hotels, houses, and streets by the ocean. She knew that there were many chicks in mountain burrows who would soon fledge and fly out to the sea.

"Dad, seabirds follow the stars to the ocean at night, and fledglings are attracted to light, right?"

"That's right, Makani."

"The chicks sometimes get confused, and fly around and around streetlights, right?"

Her dad nodded.

"Sometimes they fall to the ground. And a lot of times they're too tired to fly away, so cats and dogs eat them, or they get run over by a car!"

"Yup, all true," he said grimly.

Makani turned and glared at him. "Dad, seabirds learn so many hard things." Her voice was rising. "They learn how to find food in the huge ocean. They learn to navigate hundreds of miles over the open ocean, and they remember where to find their burrows . . ."

She crossed her arms over her chest and stared at him.

"Why can't they learn that streetlights aren't stars? *Why?*"

Her dad squinted at Makani, and then looked up at the stars and sighed. He seemed to gather himself.

Makani's eyes did not leave him.

He looked at Makani with compassion. Taking a deep breath, he spoke slowly and deliberately.

"Makani, imagine you are an ʻuaʻu. Your world is over the ocean. The only time you go to land is when you nest. For millions of years, your species has lived safely this way, nesting on islands far from predators."

All was quiet except for the sound of chirping crickets. The stars and planets shone brightly up in the sky. Makani waited.

"Then, people arrive on these islands. Soon there are buildings, poles, and wires cutting across your flight path. Artificial lights that look like stars twinkle in the night sky. These things are not part of your world! It takes a long time for animals to adapt to the changes we humans make in their environment. Sometimes it takes too long . . ."

Makani shook her head slightly. She gazed at the artificial lights by the ocean below and worried: Would HAPE#4 be OK?

Following her dad inside, Makani switched off their small outside light. She glanced briefly out the window toward the ocean before pulling down the shade.

CHAPTER TEN

BIG ISLAND, LONG MOUNTAIN

The next day, Makani and her mom headed off on an adventure that would take them to ʻuaʻu colonies on other Hawaiian islands. It was a work trip for her mom. "You'll be my assistant," she had told Makani.

Their first stop was Hawaiʻi Island, the largest and youngest of all the Hawaiian Islands, with active volcanoes still adding to its size. Mauna Loa is one of the biggest volcanic mountains in the world, and home to an ʻuaʻu colony located inside Hawaiʻi Volcanoes National Park.

Keola, the biologist monitoring wildlife in the park, was a childhood friend of Makani's mom. Her daughter, Maile, was the same age as Makani. Keola invited Makani and her mom to camp with them within the colony on Mauna Loa, to help collect ʻuaʻu data. They would be camping inside one of the largest cat-proof fences on all of the islands. The fence had been installed the year before. Everyone was excited to see if the fence was making a difference, keeping more ʻuaʻu chicks safe from predators and allowing them to fledge successfully. And Makani was excited to see Maile again. They both adored seabirds.

It was a long hike to the campsite, and it got harder when they reached higher elevations. But they had fun, chatting as they walked about the changing environment around them.

Makani marveled, "Maile! Look at that rough *ʻaʻā* lava right next to that smooth, ropey *pāhoehoe*."

"Yeah! The newer flows are so black compared to the old brown and gray flows," noted Maile. "And it's crazy that there are no tall trees up here! Look at all those scrappy little native plants, poking their heads right out of the lava!"

Makani nodded, grinning. "Right? So cool! My favorite is the *ʻōhelo!* Their berries are purply-blue up here, so different from the red and orange berries near Kīlauea Volcano."

"And they are so fat and juicy!" cried Maile. "I bet if we stayed and watched them, they'd explode right before our eyes!"

They giggled, pretending to wipe imaginary juice off their faces. They were both giddy from the high elevation and their shared enthusiasm for this adventure.

ʻŌHELO

They joined Keola and Makani's mom. As they walked together, Keola said, "In the old days, *ʻuaʻu* nested from down by the sea to all the way up here! *ʻUaʻu* were a dependable food resource. The birds came in from the sea to nest at the same time and location, year after year. Plus, they were easy to catch."

Keola stopped and pointed out a small pit before them. "*Kia manu*, bird catchers, would sometimes break away the top layer

of a deep burrow. This made it easier to harvest the *ʻuaʻu*, and it probably created more cavities for other adult birds to make burrows. Some people believe that the chicks were a delicacy and were saved for the *aliʻi*, the high chiefs to eat. But others say that mostly the chicks were harvested so the adults could return the next year and have another chick. When the *ʻuaʻu* disappeared at lower elevations, they could only be found up here, high in the mountains. And then they became rare even here."

At their campsite that evening, there was just a slight breeze, so it was chilly but not freezing. They were all cozy inside their warm jackets. Makani's mom and Keola talked quietly, weaving Hawaiian and English words into melodic, rhythmic sentences. Makani was tired, but comfortable and thoughtful. She watched the growing darkness change the look of the landscape. Stars brightened as the sky turned orange, then purple. Makani imagined thin-winged flyers following the stars over Kīlauea Volcano out to the sea. She felt a sense of belonging to this place, and to her culture. But she felt questions inside her.

There was a pause in the conversation, and Makani asked, "Aunty Keola, why did people harvest so many *ʻuaʻu?*"

Keola answered, "The *ʻuaʻu* used to be so plentiful, Makani. *Kapu* restrictions are usually an effective way to manage resources, but many things can complicate this. Luckily, these days, we have lots of other foods to eat."

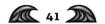

Makani hesitated, but then spoke. "At school, my friends don't know much about the 'ua'u. They say, 'things only matter when they're useful, part of our everyday lives.'"

"Yup, same with my friends," added Maile.

"Well, do things have to be useful for us to care about them?" asked Makani.

There was silence. Then, Keola spoke.

"My *makuahine*, my mother, told me about the seabirds. She learned about them from my grandmother, who learned their story from my great-grandmother, going back for many generations. My mom taught me that we humans are like seabirds in many ways! *'Ua'u* live long lives. They choose one mate, raise one chick at a time together, and work hard to keep their chick safe. They make a long, winding entrance to their deep burrow to protect their young from predators. They travel far to gather food for their chick. They take good care of their *keiki*, their child, just like your parents do for you, Makani, and like I do for you, Maile."

"The *'ua'u* are our *'aumākua*, our ancestors, our family members," Makani's mom added. "And they're in the *Kumulipo*, the creation chant, part of the fabric of life, where everything is interconnected. They hold a special place in our culture. There were once so many seabirds nesting on these islands, they darkened the skies in the evening when returning from the sea to their burrows! Hawaiians knew their ways very well."

Keola nodded. "*Ae!* But then, over time, the *'ua'u* disappeared. People thought they had gone extinct."

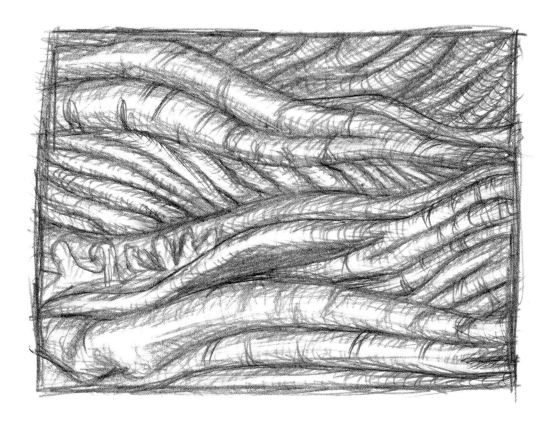

Makani's mom said, "But, lately, now that we are working to protect them, we're finding active burrows in many places!"

Everyone was quiet. Then, Keola spoke gently. "Seabirds have been nesting here in Hawai'i for millions of years. They were here long before we humans arrived. It's our *kuleana,* our responsibility, to do what we can to keep them healthy and safe . . . and that is true for *all* people from *every* culture. We humans share this *'āina* and *moana,* this land and sea, with native species. And the things we do to help them can make a difference, for them *and* for us."

A sudden gust of wind swirled around them. Just as quickly, it slowed to a gentle breeze. All was quiet and still. Stars made a brilliant, glittering mosaic across the huge sky.

Softly, Keola said, "We used to live in tune with the environment. The names of animals, plants, places, geologic features all have meaning and purpose. We need to listen to the world and remember the original names. We must try to make the connections."

Early the next morning, the sun was just starting to rise and warm the chilly air. The small plants around their camp sparkled with silvery frost. Aunty Keola and Makani's mom collected the memory cards from the cameras set up outside the burrow entrances, replacing them with new cards.

Makani and Maile's job was to look for clues showing if an ʻuaʻu nest was active. At one burrow entrance, the girls took a turn sniffing. They could both smell a faint, sweet, musky ʻuaʻu scent. Makani discovered white wash, bird poop, on many rocks around the burrow entrance. Then, Maile found a small downy feather nearby. They shone a flashlight on the ground just inside the burrow hole. "Look!" they whispered excitedly in unison. In the soft dirt at the entrance were small webbed footprints.

Keola removed the card from the wildlife camera facing the burrow's entrance and inserted it into her laptop. They watched a fuzzy video of a chick flapping furiously, resting, and then scuttling back into the burrow entrance. The girls nodded

to each other with excitement. They had found an active burrow! There was a chick sleeping inside!

Makani looked at the undulating lava landscape all around them and thought of the many lucky chicks asleep inside their burrows, safe within this fenced area.

While hiking down the mountain, Keola told them, "Last month, we brought a detection dog and his handler into the fenced area, for extra help with locating 'ua'u burrows. His name is Slater, and he is one smart, well-trained dog! Slater's handler, Mika, trained him to find the scent of 'ua'u. In the field, when Slater detects 'ua'u scent, he uses his nose like a compass to navigate to where the scent is strongest. Then he points to the source of the scent."

Keola stopped and pulled a roll of flagging tape and scissors from her backpack. "Slater needs the wind to help him detect the scent and the location of 'ua'u. On voyaging canoes, Hawaiians used *lei hulu,* a strand of chicken feathers, tied high up on the sail's mast, to see the wind direction. Now in the field, we use our own version of a *lei hulu.* We call it a telltale."

Makani, her mom, and Maile gathered around as Keola cut two lengths of the tape from the roll. She frayed one end of each piece, and then tied a telltale around each girl's wrist. The nearby plants were still,

SLATER - ONE TIRED DETECTION DOG

but when Makani held her arm up high, the telltale came to life, blowing in the gentle breeze. Makani sniffed hard, but couldn't smell anything. She imagined having a nose so strong that she could smell the scent of an *'ua'u* in the air, far from a burrow!

At their rental car, Makani and her mom hugged and said goodbye to their friends. While loading their gear into the car, Makani said, "Mom, I've been thinking . . . How about we use the Hawaiian name for HAPE#4? We could call her 'Ua'u'ehā."

Her mom's face lit up with a big smile. "'*Ae!* Yes! *Maika'i*, Makani. Good idea!" Her mom hugged her. "We'll call our petrel by her Hawaiian name, 'Ua'u'ehā."

As they pulled out of the parking lot, Makani's mom said, "Did you know that *'ehā*, the number four, had a special significance in the old days?" She glanced at Makani, who shook her head.

"These days, we count by tens, but in old Hawai'i, the counting system was connected to the number four. Many important things were grouped by fours. And the word *hā* also means 'to breathe,' and 'breath of life'!"

Makani's mom smiled. "This is a good name for our 'Ua'u'ehā."

Makani looked down thoughtfully and smiled. "To breathe." She liked the way that sounded. It made her think of the wind, and her own name.

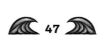

CHAPTER ELEVEN

A BROKEN WING

Makani and her mom were heading to the northernmost tip of Hawai'i Island. They traveled over the saddle, between the two massive volcanic mountains, Mauna Loa and Mauna Kea, looming on each side of the winding road.

Makani's mom said, "We'll reach the wildlife center in about an hour. When we helped Aunty Rae and Uncle Tom feed that chick on Lāna'i, the wildlife center had sent the fish slurry and got us the permits—remember?"

"Yup!" answered Makani brightly. She thought about the little chick with only one parent. "Have you heard any updates from Aunty Rae?"

"Not yet," answered her mom, squinting at the road ahead of them. "And 'Ua'u'ehā is still in her burrow at Nihokū."

Makani gazed out the window. She silently sent a positive wish to her young petrel friend.

Lisa, the wildlife center director, came out to greet them as they pulled up. "Come in and we'll tour the hospital! Then I'll introduce you to one of our patients, an *ua'u* from Maui who arrived with a broken wing."

They passed many rooms with tools and equipment for treating sick and injured native birds and bats from all around the Hawaiian archipelago. A larger room had refrigerators and freezers filled with food for their patients.

Lisa said, "Outside, we have a pool for rehabilitation, where our seabird patients exercise and get strong. They also condition their feathers there to keep them waterproof. They need to do these things before we can release them back into the wild. Our ʻuaʻu patient healed well from the broken wing bone. But, while exercising in the pool, he broke two primary flight feathers!"

"Oh, no!" cried Makani. She knew that without primary feathers an ʻuaʻu cannot fly.

"Dr. Juan was able to attach new ends to the broken feathers," said Lisa as she led them into an examination room, where Dr. Juan was examining the ʻuaʻu patient.

"He's doing great," whispered the doctor. Lisa gently spread the bird's wing feathers. Makani could hardly see where the new feather tips had been attached. She marveled at all the feathers of so many different sizes and shapes. Layered so neatly on top of one another, the feathers made beautiful, intricate patterns.

"This young bird is 'good as new!'" Lisa said. "We'll be taking him offshore to give him an easy release, with nothing between him and the ocean. Would you like to join us for his send-off?"

Makani, her mom, and Lisa stood at the shore watching the activities through binoculars. While one technician paddled the kayak, the other held the precious cargo, a bird box with the ʻuaʻu patient inside. Once they were far enough from shore, the ʻuaʻu was carefully lifted from the box. The technician held the ʻuaʻu up high in the air, facing into the wind. Suddenly, as if waking from a deep sleep, the ʻuaʻu started flapping hard.

He took to the air! But then he turned and flew inland. Makani, her mom, and Lisa ducked as the bird flew right over their heads. Turning quickly, they watched as he flew toward the mountain. Makani heard Lisa whisper, "Fly to the ocean! Please! You can do it!"

The ʻuaʻu banked in a big half circle and finally found the wind. He flapped and glided toward the sparkling water. And then he never turned back. They watched with wonder as the ʻuaʻu flew over the ocean and disappeared into the horizon.

That evening, Aunty Rae called from Lānaʻi with good news. The chick they had helped to feed had fledged! Makani realized that two ʻuaʻu had made it safely to sea that day, with help from people.

CHAPTER TWELVE

HALEAKALĀ, HOUSE OF THE SUN

The next day, they flew from Hawai'i Island to Maui. Makani gazed out the airplane window at the giant mountain rising up from the clouds. Her mom said, "My colleague Jake and his team work with the 'ua'u on Haleakalā. Jake invited us to help him band two 'ua'u chicks that are very late to fledge."

Makani glanced at her own "band" sparkling brightly in the sunlight that streamed in through the window. She gazed at the white-capped water beneath them, smiling at the thought that she was flying over the ocean . . . on metal wings!

They stood at the 10,000-foot summit atop Haleakalā— Makani, her mom, and Jake. The air was thin and sounds were strange and hollow. A stark white telescope sat on the red cinder mountain above them, fixed on the same stars that guided 'ua'u out to sea.

Makani watched her mom gently pull a sleeping chick from his burrow. The young bird squirmed and tried to bite her, but Makani's mom held the chick firmly. Jake carefully clamped a tiny metal ring on the chick's thin pink leg. Makani marveled at the chick's small, delicate-looking webbed feet. Each 'ua'u had a slightly different black design on its toes. This petrel's feet looked especially pretty to Makani. She imagined those webbed feet dashing across the surface of the ocean as the chick took to the air.

'Ua'u are often feisty, but the second chick they banded was calm. Smiling, her mom nodded to Makani to come close. Leaning in, Makani breathed in the chick's strong, musky 'ua'u scent. It was her favorite smell.

As her mom returned the chick to his burrow, Makani asked quietly, "Jake, will you build a predator-proof fence here, so the 'ua'u can be safe when they nest?"

Jake gave Makani a quizzical look. Then his expression became very serious, but his eyes were warm. Makani felt that Jake wanted to tell her something important, and he wanted her to understand. Jake spoke slowly, earnestly.

"Seabirds are amazing creatures, Makani, yet most of us don't even know that they exist." Makani nodded, listening carefully.

"Seabirds are the only vertebrates that live over the ocean. Their guano, their poop, is packed with marine nutrients, 30 percent richer than other nutrients. With their guano, seabirds feed plant communities and coral reef habitats. Seabirds help humans! They nested on the barren land and made it fertile and habitable for us before we arrived here in Hawai'i! And these birds continue to provide us with crucial ecological services. Seabirds also understand the moods of Kanaloa, god of the sea. They help sailors navigate, and help fishermen locate fish."

He shook his head, smiling. "Seabirds are so amazing!"

Jake paused, watching Makani. Then he continued.

"Have you noticed that we use fences to lock up native species? Why not focus instead on making islands safe for seabirds again? We could control our pets and invasive animals and plants; we could modify our lights, electrical cables, and windmills. Makani, have you ever thought about this?"

He tilted his head at her. "Isn't it possible to do these things?"

Jake looked steadily at Makani. His eyes sparkled and he smiled gently.

Makani was quiet, her eyes wide. She had never thought about this before. Then she nodded her head slowly. Yes! We *can* help make Hawai'i safe again for wildlife.

CHAPTER THIRTEEN

FIRST FLIGHT

Back on Kaua'i that night, the chick called 'Ua'u'ehā, HAPE#4, woke up and smelled the ocean. Every night, she had been drawn outside, exercised her wings, and explored all around her burrow, but tonight was different. Yes, she was hungry and thirsty, but she felt something more . . .

She lumbered up through the tube. Once outside, she unfolded her long thin wings and flapped. There was only a gentle breeze, but she could hear the wind and crashing waves nearby. Folding her wings, she scuttled and plodded over the uneven, rocky ground, meandering past many scrubby plants. She stopped and looked, memorizing each big rock and plant around her. But the ocean called to her, and she ventured on to find the wind.

Using her bill and wings to clamber and climb, she finally reached a high lava ledge. Waves crashed below. The wind excited her. She stretched her wings out wide again, strong from so many nights of exercise. She flapped hard. Suddenly, a gust of wind lifted her. She looked down at the land, then out to the ocean. And off she flew! Flapping, and then sailing on the powerful *makani,* she followed a path of bright stars over the sea and into the dark night sky.

CHAPTER FOURTEEN

DREAMS

Back in her own bed, Makani woke abruptly. She had been dreaming of ʻUaʻuehā. The sky was still dark and full of brilliant stars, but a glimmer of gold lit the horizon. Makani leaped out of bed and dashed down the hall to the kitchen.

Her mom was sipping coffee, staring with bleary eyes at a blurry image of a young ʻuaʻu frozen on her computer screen.

Startling her, Makani blurted from the doorway, "I dreamed ʻUaʻuehā fledged!"

Their eyes locked. Makani's mom carefully put down her coffee mug. "Let's go," she said.

They drove silently to the back entrance of the refuge. With their headlamps on, they navigated their way up the path to Nihokū. Wind blew hard and waves crashed. Their sounds mingled with the calls of ʻuaʻu

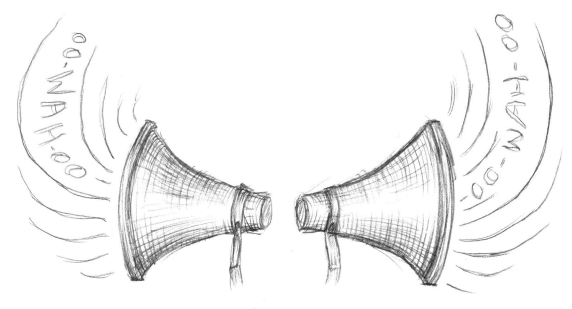

PLAYBACK SPEAKERS

playing from speakers inside the fence, a signal to wild Hawaiian petrels to come to Nihokū.

The steep path down to the row of covered burrow boxes was dimly lit by the rising sun. Makani and her mom knelt before 'Ua'u'ehā's burrow box.

Makani felt her heart thumping in her chest. Her mom snapped off the outer lid and grasped the top of the burrow box.

Makani held her breath.

Her mom lifted the top.

'Ua'u'ehā was gone.

Makani stood. She looked down at her mom, whose eyes shone up at Makani, barely visible in the dim light. Makani felt her heart squeeze.

She turned and followed the path that ʻUaʻuʻehā had taken, walking over the same shrubs that the ʻuaʻu had scuttled around. Makani climbed up onto the lava ledge, standing where the young seabird had stood in her dream.

The ocean was huge and thunderously loud before her.

Makani whispered, "Be safe, ʻUaʻuʻehā. I hope you find lots of good food to eat out there." The words caught in her throat.

"Someday, let's meet here again at Nihokū!"

EPILOGUE
Finding Home

Five years passed and four more cohorts of Hawaiian petrel chicks had been translocated from their mountain burrows and raised at Nihokū. The chicks had all fledged successfully, and the team had celebrated joyfully. But, as each season passed and no ʻuaʻu returned, the concerns of the team grew.

What if none of the fledglings came back to Nihokū?

What if the project failed?

ʻUaʻu numbers were steeply declining in the wild . . . The team waited nervously, hoping.

Makani was now sixteen years old.

It was spring, early morning. She found her mom in the kitchen pouring hot tea into three to-go mugs. Her mom looked like she hadn't slept much in a long, long time.

WING AND TAIL RULER

Without looking up, she said, "Bobby just texted. He said we should come down. All of us. Now."

Her voice was flat, her words clipped.

Makani could see the worry in her mom's eyes. Makani's stomach jumped nervously. They piled into the truck—Makani, her mom, and her dad—and drove in silence to Nihokū.

Bobby was sitting in the shed, looking at his laptop when they arrived.

"You have to see this."

He turned the laptop toward them. There was a dim view of the inside of a burrow box. Bobby sharpened the image as they all leaned in.

"Is there a bird in there?" her mom asked, squinting at the screen.

Bobby said, "Wait."

As he enlarged the picture, Makani felt her heart start to beat more quickly. There, peeking out from under black wing feathers, was a little pink ʻuaʻu ankle with a band on it.

Makani's breath caught in her throat.

It was ʻUaʻuʻehā.

Suddenly, she felt her eyes well up. She quickly wiped the tears away. Her mom turned to look at Makani, wiping her own eyes and smiling. They hugged, laughing with relief and happiness.

"She came back!" Makani whispered to her mom.

"*Ae!* Our ʻUaʻuʻehā!" her mom whispered back.

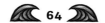

Holding Makani before her, she looked into her daughter's eyes. She shook her head and smiled. "The last of her cohort to leave, and the first 'ua'u to return to Nihokū!"

Makani's dad pulled them both into a big embrace. Then, Bobby stood and gave everyone a grand high five. With great gusto, he said, "She'll head off soon, maybe show up again next year or the year after, meet another petrel, fall in love, and raise a chick in one of these deluxe condos we built for them."

Everyone laughed. Bobby stretched and yawned. "Meanwhile, we won't disturb her. And we'll keep our fingers crossed that other petrels show up soon."

Back home in her room that evening, Makani felt exhausted and exhilarated at the same time. She looked through her field journal, at the sketches and notes she'd been keeping since the start of the translocation project. Makani had learned so much about the 'ua'u since those magical nights on Lāna'i when she was just a small child. She felt lucky that she had grown up with seabirds as part of her world.

Makani marveled at how 'Ua'u'ehā lived in a world so different from her own, yet she felt such a strong connection to this wild bird. As Makani herself prepared to "fledge" and go off-island to college, she knew this connection would be a comfort to her as she followed her own path, alone, into a new world. Makani would look forward to updates from Nihokū.

"Others will return," she said out loud. "I know they will."

Makani closed her journal. Gazing at the metal bracelet on her wrist, she thought about how dangerous we had made the world for nesting seabirds. Then, she remembered all the people who were working to help the ʻuaʻu: her mom's team and partners here on Kauaʻi; Aunty Rae and Uncle Tom on Lānaʻi; Aunty Keola, Lisa, and her team at the wildlife center on Hawaiʻi Island; Jake and his team on Maui . . .

Makani whispered, "There are many things we can *all* do to make Hawaiʻi safer for seabirds. Even little things make a difference!"

She sighed. The words of Aunty Keola and Jake echoed in her mind: *Most people don't even know about the seabirds.*

Makani stared out the window into the darkness.

She whispered, "If only I could tell the story of the seabirds. Then, people everywhere would know about the ʻuaʻu, and our connection to them!"

An idea was starting to take shape inside her. Her mind raced, her thoughts flying around wildly like wings flapping in the still air.

But then, Makani closed her eyes. She took in a slow, steadying breath. She imagined spreading her wings and soaring over the sea in the night sky. Suddenly, a path of stars appeared before her! Makani smiled, and then she followed that path of stars.

She opened her eyes, reached for her journal, and found her pencil inside.

And then, Makani began to write.

Once upon a time, petrels filled the night skies of Hawai'i . . .

And as Makani wrote, 'Ua'u'ehā, HAPE#4, was taking off again from Nihokū. The young petrel knew nothing of her name, of cats, dogs, rats, artificial lights, buildings, poles, and wires. The *'ua'u* knew only the wonderful feeling of the wind and soaring over the sea, the smells of the ocean with good food beneath the surface, the feel of cool water under her webbed feet, and the bright stars that guided her.

One day, she would again feel the call to Nihokū, to find a mate and raise young of her own. But, finally, 'Ua'u'ehā had found her true home . . . over the sea.

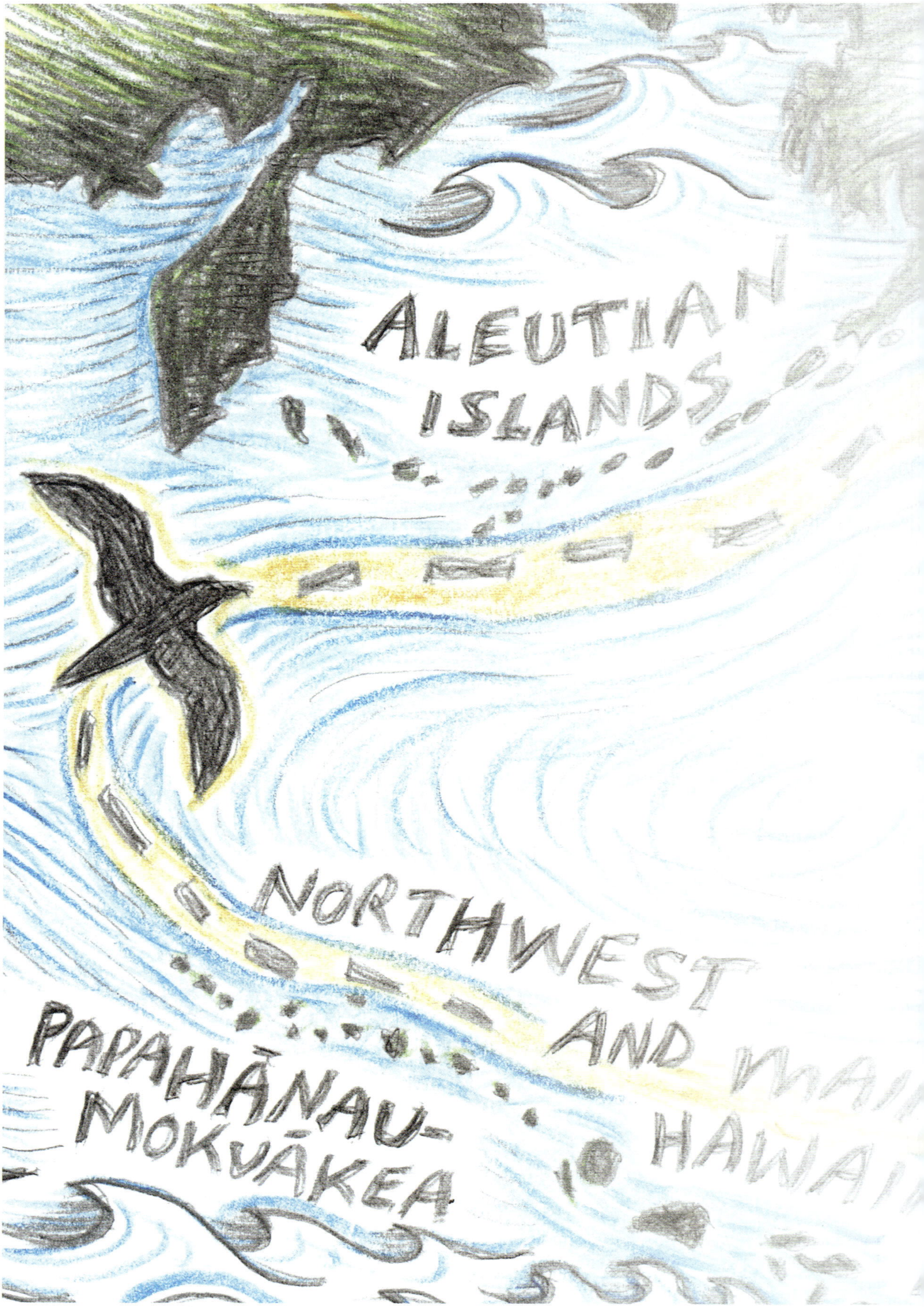
ALEUTIAN
ISLANDS
NORTHWEST
AND
HAWAI
PAPAHĀNAU-
MOKUĀKEA

A HAWAIIAN PETREL'S JOURNEY

THE STORY BEHIND THE STORY

THE TRANSLOCATION PROJECT AT NIHOKŪ

I have been lucky to spend time in ‘ua‘u colonies, on Lāna‘i, Maui, Hawai‘i Island, and at Nihokū on Kaua‘i. Many amazing people are working hard to save seabirds in Hawai‘i, and they taught me so much. The ‘ua‘u, and the powerful experiences these "seabird people" shared with me, inspired this story.

      Over five years, 106 Hawaiian petrels have been raised and fledged in the translocation program at Nihokū. As of 2022, eight of the translocated ‘ua‘u had returned to the artificial burrows, and three pairs had nested there. Finally, in November 2022, the very first Hawaiian petrel chick that was hatched by translocated parents fledged from Nihokū! Now, seventy-six artificial burrows inside the predator-exclusion fence await the return of other translocated chicks, and maybe wild birds, too. Nihokū has the potential to become a thriving nesting colony, providing a safe haven for diverse nesting seabird species into the future.

WHAT ARE HAWAIIAN PETRELS, ʻUAʻU?

ʻUaʻu (oo-WAH-oo), Hawaiian petrels, are highly pelagic seabirds, living their lives mostly over the ocean. They fly using very little energy, night and day, powered by the wind. They soar and glide over huge distances. With their incredible superpower senses, they are guided to food, to their colonies, and to their burrows. They use smell and an inner magnetic map, and they have the capacity to see ultraviolet and possibly even infrared wavelengths. The only time their webbed feet touch land is when they meet their life mate at their burrow to raise one chick per season.

Photo courtesy of Rachel Sprague.

CHICK

Photo courtesy of Rachel Sprague.

FLEDGLING

Photo courtesy of Bret Nainoa Mossman.

ADULT

It may seem strange that a bird of the sea nests on land, in a hole in the ground high in the mountains. But, for the last sixty million years, this lifestyle worked well for ʻuaʻu—finding food all around the Pacific Ocean, and nesting on remote islands where they were safe from predators. ʻUaʻu and other seabirds have played an important role in Hawaiʻi's ecosystem by bringing marine nutrients to land. Through the ages, from their burrows high in the mountains, seabird guano, poop, has washed down the volcanic slopes, through the forests, all the way to the sea. This guano has nourished the land and the offshore coral reefs, and has added immensely to the fertility and growth of island flora, fauna, coral, and ocean life. Seabirds helped to make Hawaiʻi the green, fertile place that it was when the first humans arrived, and they continue to do so.

FACTS ABOUT
THE ʻUAʻU

- Endemic to Hawaiʻi (nesting nowhere else in the world)
- Scientific name: *Pterodroma* (Greek for "winged runner") *sandwichensis*
- Family: Procellariidae
- Status: endangered; International Union for Conservation of Nature (IUCN) Red List: vulnerable
- Body length: 16"
- Wing span: about 36"
- Wing shape: long, thin, and pointed
- Feathers: adult plumage mostly dark feathers above with white feathers below; distinctive black "hood" with white forehead; hatchling and chick plumage very fluffy and light gray down, lighter on chest and belly

- Legs: pink
- Feet: webbed feet and toes, pink with black on the tips
- Beaks: hooked, sharp tipped for grabbing prey
- Flight: dynamic soaring; exploit the wind over the ocean to glide efficiently over long distances, using little energy. With wings outstretched, they glide in high smooth arcs, turn side to side, and go up and down, like a flying sailboat
- Sleep: sleep while flying, able to "turn off" and rest half their brain at a time
- Mature late; can live forty-six years or more
- Live over the ocean and only come to land to mate
- After fledging, might visit natal colony after three or four years at sea; after five years, begin prospecting for a mate
- Mate for life
- Return to same island, to the same nest site or area yearly
- Able to remember locations of favorite fishing grounds, thousands of miles away over open ocean, and navigate back to nests on tiny islands
- Nocturnal, only active at night in their breeding colony

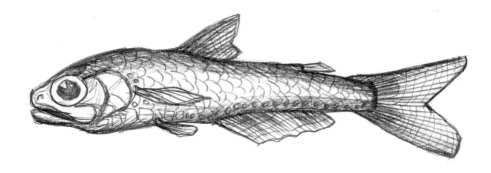

WHAT DO ʻUAʻU EAT AND DRINK, AND HOW DO THEY CATCH THEIR PREY?

- Favorite foods: squid; also eat juvenile goatfish, squirrelfish, lantern fish, and hatchetfish
- "Tube-nosed": glands in their tubelike nostrils enable them to drink seawater by filtering out the salt and then sneezing out droplets of salty brine; also get water from the fish they eat
- Feeding styles: "surface seizing"—grab food prey while floating, and "contact dipping"—fly low and catch fish while in flight
- Hunt day and night using sight and smell to find food
- Commonly hunt at night when food prey migrate up to the surface
- Many prey are bioluminescent and can be seen in the dark
- Hunt in mixed flocks with other seabird species
- Often follow schools of predators like tuna, mahimahi, porpoises, dolphins, and whales that hunt at deeper depths and drive smaller fish up to the surface

NESTING TIME!
BREEDING ACTIVITIES
AND SCHEDULES

WHERE DO ʻUAʻU NEST?

Historically, ʻuaʻu were abundant, with huge colonies found from the sea to the mountaintops on all of the Hawaiian Islands. But now they are rare, found only on mountains at higher elevations. Known ʻuaʻu colonies at the time of the writing of this book include:

- **Maui** at the summit of Haleakalā
- **Lānaʻi** in Lānaʻihale
- **Kauaʻi** in Hono O Nā Pali Natural Area Reserve and Upper Limahuli Preserve
- **Hawaiʻi Island** on Mauna Kea, Mauna Loa, and in the Kohala Mountains

HOW DO ʻUAʻU MAKE AND THEN FIND THEIR BURROW?

ʻUaʻu nest inside a burrow. Depending on the terrain, the ʻuaʻu make their burrow in different ways:

- Excavate burrows inside rock crevices, in wet, dense forests
- Excavate burrows on steep, dry slopes
- Use existing lava tubes or crevices in old lava flows
- Burrow size and shape depends on the natural shape of the hole or lava tube
- ʻUaʻu find their burrow easily, even at night in total darkness, using olfaction (smell) and sight, zooming in at 31–37 mph, landing near their burrow entrance, and scuttling inside

The timing for breeding activities and schedules is slightly different for each island colony. The ʻuaʻu on Haleakalā, Maui, arrive at their colony first, more than a month earlier than the other islands' colonies. On other islands, ʻuaʻu start the season later but then follow similar timing from the first arrival of adults to the fledging of chicks.

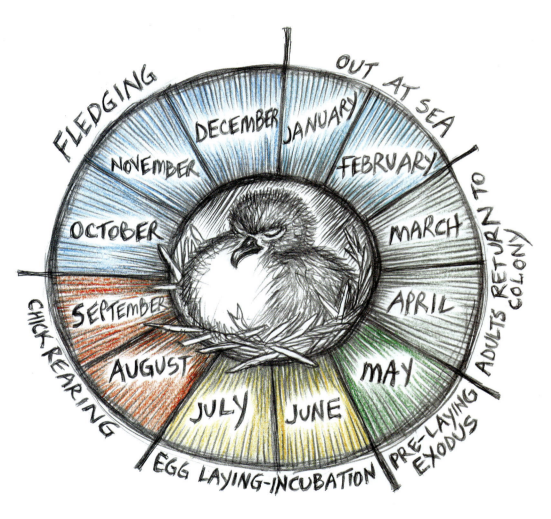

MAUI ʻUAʻU
BREEDING CALENDAR

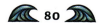

GENERAL CALENDAR OF 'UA'U BREEDING SEASON
FOR ALL ISLAND COLONIES

February through August (Maui);
March through November (Lāna'i, Kaua'i, Hawai'i):

- Adults arrive at the natal colony, engage in aerial flights, reconnect with their mate or prospect for a new mate. On Haleakalā, unattached males sometimes sit at a burrow entrance waiting for a female to select them as their mate

- It takes several seasons to dig out a burrow, or establish a nest in an existing cavity like a lava tube or crevice. Once established, they always nest in the same burrow. Each year, adults clean and sometimes excavate the burrow more

- Nesting materials vary depending on the individual bird and the surrounding plants. They sometimes drag dried leaves, twigs, or stems into the burrow for their nest, but sometimes they do not use any materials and simply nest on the soft ground

- Longer tubes to the burrows mean there is less temperature change inside burrows; deeper burrows are safer for chicks, and also for adults, who are extremely vulnerable to predation during incubation

March/April (Maui);
May/June (Lāna'i, Kaua'i, Hawai'i):

- After mating, both adults leave for a three-week "pre-laying exodus" to eat and shore up energy

April/May (Maui);
June/July (Lānaʻi, Kauaʻi, Hawaiʻi):

- Female returns to the burrow, lays one egg—chalky white color; heavy, weighing 18 percent of the mother's weight (the human equivalent would be a 125-pound woman giving birth to a 22.5-pound baby!)
- Sometimes, the female leaves right after laying the egg. If the male is there, he begins incubating immediately, or he arrives soon after to incubate the egg. The egg can be left for up to three days before it has to be incubated, but once incubation starts, it must be continuous
- The couple takes turns incubating the egg for about fifty-two days

May/June (Maui);
July/August/September (Lānaʻi, Kauaʻi, Hawaiʻi):

- Chick hatches with one adult in attendance. Sometimes, while the chick is emerging, the adult will help by moving the egg to a better position
- Chick is kept warm for a few days until it can thermoregulate—maintain its own body temperature
- Both adults then leave to gather fresh fish and squid, which provide nutrition and water for the chick. Parents produce a stomach oil from the squid and fish that they catch. They feed the chick through regurgitation
- Parents alternate between short foraging trips of one or two days and longer trips of up to three weeks
- Chick is fed by adults for 100–115 days

October (Maui);
November/December (Lānaʻi, Kauaʻi, Hawaiʻi):

- Chick fledges, flying to the ocean to begin life on its own

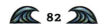

SEABIRDS IN HAWAIIAN CULTURE

In the days of old Hawai'i, seabirds held an important place in life, and people understood their ways.

- It was known that some seabirds, like terns and noddies, fed in waters close to shore when provisioning for their young, returning to their land nests with fish for their hungry chicks. People out at sea counted on these birds to guide them to land. About 1,500 years ago, seabirds helped voyagers navigate to and settle on the Hawaiian Islands

- Seabirds were watched closely, as they gave clues about coming changes in weather patterns

- The *ka'upu*—black-footed albatross—and other albatross species are considered body forms or *kino lau* of Lono, the agricultural deity, and played a part in the yearly Makahiki Festival, celebrating fertility in the land

- Feathers of forest birds and some seabirds (especially the *'iwa*, the frigatebird) were used in making *kāhili* (feather standards), *lei hulu* (feather necklaces), *'ahu'ula* (long feathered capes worn by the *ali'i nui*, the high chief), *kīpuka* (shorter feathered capes worn by lower ranking *ali'i*), *akua hulu manu* (feather god images), and *mahiole* (feather helmets)

KĀHILI, FEATHER STANDARD

- Fishermen looking for schools of big fish follow petrels and shearwaters; the birds track schools of big fish when hunting for the little fish they eat, which are driven up from the depths by the larger fish the fishermen are looking for

MAKAU, FISH HOOK

'UA'U AS A FOOD RESOURCE

'Ua'u used to be plentiful and common in Hawai'i. They made their nesting burrows at sea level and all the way up the mountains. During nesting season, the skies were said to blacken when the seabirds returned to their burrows at the end of the day. The 'ua'u were an important and reliable food resource for some people. Some say that adult 'ua'u were eaten by commoners, and young birds were a delicacy saved for the *ali'i nui*, the high chiefs. Others say that only the chicks would be taken, to preserve the adult population so they could lay eggs again the next breeding season.

Kia manu, bird catchers in old Hawai'i, would go to the cold and barren high Hawai'i mountains. There, 'ua'u were easy to find and catch; 'ua'u nested in big colonies and returned to the same burrows every year. People modified nesting pits for easier access to the birds in their burrows and possibly to help create access to new nesting burrows for other 'ua'u.

'UA'U CAPTURE TECHNIQUES

- *Kono manu:* attracting the attention of a bird by imitating its call. 'Ua'u were named after their nocturnal call, which sounds exactly like their name: "oo-wah-oo"

- *Kono:* removing a bird from a burrow using a long stick with a hooked piece attached at the end, usually made of 'ie'ie roots. The end piece was covered in sticky *kēpau,* a glue-like substance made from the sap of plants like 'ulu (breadfruit), 'ōhā/hāhā (clermontia), 'akoko (euphorbia), and others

- *Lawai'amanu:* using wide nets to catch adult birds on their return path from the ocean at night (literally "to fish birds")

- Using a forked stick to reach inside a burrow, and twisting the stick to entangle the downy feathers of a chick

- Reaching a hand into a shallow burrow

- Attracting and disorienting birds with fires

WHAT ARE THE MAIN THREATS TO SEABIRDS?

The world became dangerous for seabirds nesting on remote islands when humans arrived there. Studies of fossil bird bones found in historic kitchen middens reveal that many species of birds and plants were already extinct by the time early Western explorers arrived in Hawai'i. The decline of endemic animals and plants escalated with the arrival of many more humans.

PREDATORS AND DISTURBANCE

- Cats are the number one threat to the survival of seabirds and all birds around the world. Although we may not think of our pets as predators, free-roaming cats kill nearly 2.4 billion birds every year

- Off-leash dogs disturb, injure, or kill nesting seabirds

- Mongoose, rats, and mice eat eggs and disturb nesting seabirds

- Other free-ranging animals introduced by humans that are dangerous to nesting seabirds include ungulates (hooved animals) like goats and pigs, which crush burrows and sometimes eat chicks

ARTIFICIAL LIGHTS, WIRES, AND BUILDINGS

Young seabirds fledge at night, leaving their nests to fly away from the land and begin their life over the sea. They are guided by the moon and the stars to the ocean, but can be confused by artificial lights, circling the lights until they fall to the ground exhausted. These downed seabirds are called "fallout." Seabirds of all ages also collide with utility poles, wires, and buildings. Once on the ground, downed birds are usually injured or stunned and not able to take off again, becoming easy prey for predators and vulnerable to dehydration, starvation, and being hit by cars.

HABITAT LOSS

- Land development has caused the loss of nesting habitat for seabirds, and human construction activities disturb nearby nesting seabirds
- Introduced invasive plants that have no natural enemies take over areas where native plants used to grow, affecting many native birds. The main invasive plants that displace nesting habitat include strawberry guava, Australian tree fern, and Kahili ginger

WIND TURBINES

Wind is a good source of renewable energy, but many wind turbines are placed in the flight paths of seabirds, migrating birds, and bats, who use wind corridors for travel. The big blades and tall structures of traditional wind turbines kill many flying creatures. There is ongoing research for new technologies that would make wind energy bird safe.

FINDING FOOD AT SEA, AND PLASTIC

- Industrial fishing has been taking place for the past one hundred years around Hawai'i and is affecting the diets of Hawaiian petrels

- Pieces of plastic are being found in the stomachs and burrows of 'ua'u and nearly all seabird species

- Seabirds and marine mammals also get tangled in or injured by plastic debris in the ocean

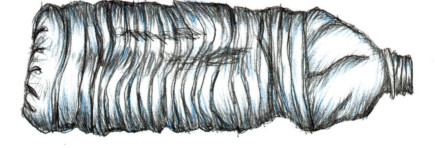

HOW DO BIOLOGISTS HELP HAWAIIAN PETRELS?

'Ua'u and their burrows can be difficult for biologists to find. Here are some ways that biologists look for *'ua'u*, locate their burrows, attract more birds to a good nesting area, and make decisions about how to manage a colony:

- Similar habitat: explore areas with similar habitats to those in known nesting locations
- Archeological sites: visit areas that have human modified pits, where humans once interacted with seabirds
- Visit known seabird locations: where diurnal seabirds have already been seen or heard, there might also be nocturnal species
- Night auditory surveys: listen for bird vocalizations at night
- Night vision: use special goggles to see birds at night
- Song meters: record audio of birds. It can often be heard in these recordings if a bird is calling from the ground or from the air. More frequent calls may indicate a nearby nest, more breeding birds, and/or how big a colony is. The number of calls can indicate bird population size and help with management of the area

- Identify active nests: "white wash" (poop), adult feathers, chick down, seabird scent, and footprints all indicate that an 'ua'u has visited recently or may be nesting nearby. Sometimes toothpicks are stuck into the ground at the entrance to a burrow. If the tooth-picks are knocked down or missing, an 'ua'u may have entered or exited the burrow, or even taken the toothpicks inside to use as nesting material

- Detection dogs: they are carefully trained to recognize seabird scents and locate active nests with their keen sense of smell

- Wildlife cameras: placed at one or more entrances to a known or possible burrow, the cameras are motion triggered to take a photo and/or a video, recording incoming or outgoing birds and preda-tors, and a chick fledging

- Burrow scopes: used to peek inside burrows to check if there are nesting adults and chicks

- Predator-exclusion fence: a fence built to keep out introduced animals that prey on native birds. Some fences are designed for cats, some for ungulates, and some for all non-native mammalian predators, including cats, dogs, pigs, mongooses, rats, and mice

- Social attraction: "playback units" (used only in areas that are protected from predators) broadcast *ʻuaʻu* calls in places where *ʻuaʻu* might be visiting, and can often attract more birds to the site

AN EXAMPLE OF HOW THESE TOOLS CAN BE USED TOGETHER

High on a remote mountain, biologists visit an area where there are human-modified pits, and old stories tell that *ʻuaʻu* used to nest there. A series of song meters are set up in a row, going down a lava flow. The song meters record many *ʻuaʻu*, calling as they fly across the landscape. Biologists then survey the area with a detection dog and its handler. At night, the biologists hear *ʻuaʻu* calls, and see them through night-vision goggles. During the day, with the help of the detection dog, they discover three nests.

Wildlife cameras are set up at the nest entrances, or a burrow scope is used, to confirm that birds are visiting and the nest is active. If the area is already protected from predators with a fence, playback units are set up to play *ʻuaʻu* vocalizations. Hopefully, these calls will attract more *ʻuaʻu* to this protected area and let wild birds know that this is a good nesting location.

HOW CAN WE HELP SEABIRDS?

Many native species are in trouble, but there are many things that we can do to help them. ʻUaʻu and other seabirds respond quickly to our assistance. We can all be partners in helping seabirds. Here's how:

- Keep your pet cats and dogs indoors, and on leashes or within fences when outside.

- From September through December, which is "fallout season" in Hawaiʻi (when seabird chicks are fledging), turn off your porch lights and landscape lighting and close all curtains in the evening, so birds are not attracted to the artificial lights and can follow the moon and stars with less distraction

- Replace outdoor lights with directional lighting; point lights down and away from the beach and replace bright outdoor lighting with lower-intensity lights

- Use less plastic by bringing your own to-go containers and refuse plastic utensils and straws at restaurants. Use your own refillable coffee cup and water bottle. Recycle or dispose of used fishing line in designated disposal areas so it doesn't go into the ocean
- Pick up plastic on your local beaches so less plastic ends up in the ocean, where seabirds and other wildlife might mistake it for food
- Eat fish from markets and restaurants that use sustainable fishing methods. Learn which seafoods have less of an impact on the environment from a reliable source such as the Monterey Bay Aquarium's Seafood Watch Program
- Encourage hotels and businesses to point lights down and shield them on top, and use special bulbs with lower frequencies that don't attract birds and other wildlife
- Encourage utility companies to put reflective tape and hang reflective discs on wires, or install laser light beams next to wires, to make them more visible to birds so they avoid flying into the wires
- Support organizations that help seabirds and other wildlife
- Volunteer with organizations that work with seabirds and other wildlife
- Learn more about the seabirds in your area
- Share with others what you learn

WHAT IF YOU FIND A FALLEN SEABIRD?

One of the following organizations can help:

- The Department of Land and Natural Resources: https://dlnr.hawaii.gov/wildlife/seabird-fallout-season
- On Kauaʻi, Save Our Shearwaters: https://saveourshearwaters.org
- On Maui, Maui Nui Seabird Recovery Project: https://mauinuiseabirds.org
- On Oʻahu, Oʻahu Seabird Group: https://oahuseabirdgroup.org
- On Hawaiʻi Island, Hawaiʻi Wildlife Center: https://www.hawaiiwildlifecenter.org
- Or call the animal hospital, humane society, or seabird organization near you

ENDEMIC AND INDIGENOUS SEABIRDS OF HAWAI'I

(COMMON, SCIENTIFIC, AND HAWAIIAN NAMES)

ENDEMIC SEABIRDS
(birds that nest only in Hawai'i)

Many different kinds of seabirds nest on the Hawaiian Islands, but only two species are endemic, nesting exclusively in Hawai'i: Hawaiian petrels and Newell's shearwaters. Both of these species eat squid and fish, but they have very different ways of hunting: 'ua'u, Hawaiian petrels, are surface eaters, while 'a'o, Newell's shearwaters, are divers, using their wings to "fly" underwater and chase their prey to depths of almost 150 feet! Newell's shearwaters are critically endangered, and on the IUCN (International Union for Conservation of Nature) Red List of Threatened Species.

'UA'U
SURFACE SEIZING

Shearwaters and Petrels

Newell's shearwater
Puffinus newelli / ʻAʻo

Hawaiian petrel
Pterodroma sandwichensis / ʻUaʻu

ʻAʻo,
NEWELL'S SHEARWATER

ʻAʻO DIVING

INDIGENOUS SEABIRDS
(birds that nest in Hawaiʻi and elsewhere)

There are many species of seabirds that came on their own to nest in Hawaiʻi, and also nest in other places.

Albatrosses

Laysan albatross
Phoebastria immutabilis / Mōlī

Black-footed albatross
Phoebastria nigripes / Kaʻupu

Short-tailed albatross
Phoebastria albatrus /
Kaʻupuʻākala and Makalena

KAʻUPU,
BLACK-FOOTED ALBATROSS

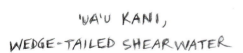

ʻUAʻU KANI,
WEDGE-TAILED SHEARWATER

Shearwaters and Petrels

Wedge-tailed shearwater
Ardenna pacifica / ʻUaʻu kani

Christmas shearwater
Puffinus nativitatis / ʻAoʻū

Bulwer's petrel
Bulweria bulwerii / ʻOu

Bonin petrel
Pterodroma hypoleuca / Nunulu

Storm-Petrels

Band-rumped storm-petrel
Hydrobates castro / ʻAkēʻakē

Tristram's storm-petrel
Hydrobates tristrami / ʻAkihikeʻehiʻale

ʻAKĒ ʻAKĒ,
BAND-RUMPED STORM-PETREL

KOAʻE ʻULA,
RED-TAILED TROPICBIRD

Tropicbirds

Red-tailed tropicbird
Phaethon rubricauda / Koaʻe ʻUla

White-tailed tropicbird
Phaethon lepturus / Koaʻe Kea

 99

2024-01-Coated, TPGX CMYK Round

0701

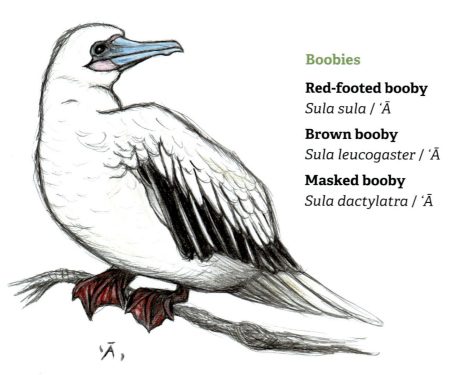

'Ā,

RED-FOOTED BOOBY

Boobies

Red-footed booby
Sula sula / 'Ā

Brown booby
Sula leucogaster / 'Ā

Masked booby
Sula dactylatra / 'Ā

Terns and Noddies

Sooty tern
Onychoprion fuscatus / 'Ewa'ewa

Gray-backed tern
Onychoprion lunatus / Pākalakala

White tern
Gygis alba / Manu-o-Kū

Brown noddy
Anous stolidus / Noio Kōhā

Black noddy
Anous minutus / Noio

Blue-gray noddy
Anous ceruleus / Hinaokū and Manuohina

MANU-O-KŪ,

WHITE TERN

Great frigatebird
Fregata minor / ʻIwa

ʻIWA,
GREAT FRIGATEBIRD

THE PEOPLE
AND GROUPS
WHO INSPIRED
THIS STORY

Kauaʻi: Project partners for the Nihokū Ecosystem Restoration Project (which includes the *ʻuaʻu* translocation program): the United States Fish and Wildlife Service and Kīlauea Point National Wildlife Refuge, Pacific Rim Conservation, the Kauaʻi Endangered Seabird Recovery Project (the Hawaiʻi Division of Land and Natural Resources and the Pacific Cooperative Studies Unit of the University of Hawaiʻi), American Bird Conservancy, the National Fish and Wildlife Foundation, the Hawaiʻi Department of Land and Natural Resources Division of Forestry and Wildlife, Kauaʻi Natural Area Reserves System, the Kauaʻi Island Utility Cooperative, the National Tropical Botanical Garden, and the David and Lucille Packard Foundation Marine Birds Program; and Archipelago Research and Conservation

Lānaʻi: Pulama Lānaʻi

Maui: Maui Nui Seabird Recovery Project; and Haleakalā National Park

Hawaiʻi Island: Pacific Cooperative Studies Unit, University of Hawaiʻi, Mānoa, at Hawaiʻi Volcanoes National Park; and Hawaiʻi Wildlife Center

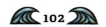

GLOSSARY OF HAWAIIAN WORDS

'a'ā. A rough chunky lava

'ae. Yes

'ahu'ula. Long feathered capes worn by *ali'i nui*

'āina. Land

'akoko. Euphorbia, an endemic Hawaiian plant

akua hulu manu. Feather god images

ali'i nui. High chief

'aumākua. Ancestors

'āwīwī. To hurry; be speedy, swift, quick

'ehā. Four

hā. To breathe; exhale; breath, life; also the number four

hāhā or *'ōhā.* Clermontia; an endemic Hawaiian lobelia plant that produces beautiful flowers

holoholo. To go for a walk

hulu. Feather

'ie'ie. An endemic Hawaiian plant with a woody vine

'iwa. Frigatebird

kāhili. Feather standard, symbolic of royalty

kapu. Taboo, prohibition

ka'upu. Black-footed albatross

kēpau. A sticky substance derived from plants, used for pulling chicks from burrows

kia manu. Bird catcher

kino lau. Body form

kīpuka. Short feathered cape or cloak worn by lower ranking *ali'i*

kono manu. To attract the attention of a bird by imitating its call

kumulipo. Origin, source of life; the name of a Hawaiian creation chant

lawai'amanu. To catch birds in the air with wide nets (literally "to fish birds")

lei hulu. Feather necklace, worn for decoration, and also used on voyaging canoes to show wind direction and the speed of the canoe

mahiole. Feather helmet

maika'i. Good

Makahiki. A yearly festival celebrating fertility in the land

makani. Wind

makau. Fishhook

makuahine. Mother

moana. Ocean

pāhoehoe. A smooth, unbroken kind of lava, braided looking

'Ua'u'ehā. Literally "Fourth Hawaiian Petrel"

'ulu. Breadfruit

uluhe. An indigenous Hawaiian fern that grows to form dense thickets

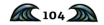

GLOSSARY OF ENGLISH WORDS

archipelago. A group of islands

bioluminescence. The emission of light from living organisms

brood. Sit on an egg to incubate, keeping it warm

clutch. A batch of eggs in one nest

cohort. A group of individuals born during the same time period

colony. A group of birds that nest together

diurnal. Active during the daytime

dynamic soaring. An efficient form of flight over the ocean, using the wind to glide—with wings outstretched—in high smooth arcs, turning side to side, going up and down

ecosystem. An area where the animals, plants, and other life-forms work together with the weather and the land to form a unique place where all things are dependent on one another

endemic. In the case of seabirds, nesting exclusively in one region

fauna. Animals of a region

feral. Wild, especially if previously domesticated

flagging tape. A lightweight tape often used for marking boundaries

fledge. To develop wing feathers and take flight

flora. Plants of a region

incubate. Sit on an egg, keeping it warm until the chick inside hatches

indigenous. In the case of seabirds, nesting in more than one region

infrared wavelengths. A kind of light that is invisible to the human eye

midden. Garbage heap from a historic cooking area where humans piled their waste materials, including bones

nocturnal. Active only at night

olfaction. The sense of smell

pelagic. In the case of birds, spending most of their lives over the ocean, and only on land when they are nesting

plumage. Birds' feathers

provision. Supply with food or drink

regurgitate. To bring up partially digested food

thermoregulate. Keep one's own body temperature warm or cool

translocate. Move from one place to another

ultraviolet wavelength. A kind of light that is invisible to the human eye

ungulate. Hooved animal

RESOURCES

Online Resources

Pacific Rim Conservation: https://pacificrimconservation.org

Maui Nui Seabird Recovery Project: https://mauinuiseabirds.org

Hawai'i Wildlife Center: https://www.hawaiiwildlifecenter.org

Kaua'i Endangered Seabird Recovery Project: https://kauaiseabirdproject.org

Cornell Lab of Ornithology. "Hawaiian Petrel." Birds of the World.
    https://birdsoftheworld.org/bow/species/hawpet1/cur/introduction

Cornell Lab of Ornithology. "Hawaiian Petrel—Pterodroma sandwichensis." eBird.
    https://media.ebird.org/catalog?taxonCode=hawpet1

Desai, Aditi. "Video: Hawaiian Petrels Journey to Safety." *American Bird Conservancy,*
    Bird Calls Blog (blog), March 3, 2016. https://abcbirds.org/video-hawaiian-petrels-journey.
    (A four-minute movie that chronicles conservationists' daring efforts to move nestling
    petrels to a predator-free area where they will hopefully start a new colony.)

Books about the Seabirds of Hawai'i and Hawaiian Cultural Practices

Harrison, Craig. *Seabirds of Hawaii: Natural History and Conservation.* Ithaca, NY: Comstock/
    Cornell University Press, 1990.

Kamakau, Samuel M. *The Works of the People of Old: Nā Hana a ka Po'e Kahiko.* Bernice P. Bishop
    Museum Special Publication 61. Honolulu: Bishop Museum Press, 1992.

Shallenberger, Robert. *Hawaiian Birds of the Sea: Nā Manu Kai.* Honolulu: University of Hawai'i
    Press, 2010.

Deeper Explorations: Scientific Papers, Books, and Presentations

Adams, J., D. G. Ainley, J. F. Penniman, C. Bailey, J. Tamayose, F. Duvall, and H. Freifeld. "Anti-
    Cyclonic Circulation and the Long-Range Foraging Movements of Hawaiian Petrels
    (Pterodroma Sandwichensis) in the North Pacific." Pacific Seabird Group Annual Meeting,
    Honolulu, 2012. http://www.pacificseabirdgroup.org/2012mtg/PSG2012.AbstractBook.pdf.

Banko, Winston E. *History of Endemic Hawaiian Birds, Part I. Population Histories—Species*
    Accounts, Sea Birds: Hawaiian Dark-Rumped Petrel ('Ua'u). Honolulu: Cooperative National
    Park Resources Studies Unit, University of Hawai'i at Mānoa, Department of Botany, 1980.
    https://scholarspace.manoa.hawaii.edu/items/86209593-5d4b-4469-8170-3fc8749496b5.

Beckwith, Martha W. *Kepelino's Traditions of Hawaii.* Bernice P. Bishop Museum Bulletin 95.
    Honolulu: Bishop Museum Press, 2007.

———. *The Kumulipo: A Hawaiian Creation Chant.* Honolulu: University of Hawai'i Press, 1972.

Berger, Andrew. *Hawaiian Birdlife.* 2nd ed. Honolulu: University of Hawai'i Press, 1981.

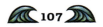

Duffy, David Cameron. "Changing Seabird Management in Hawai'i: From Exploitation through Management to Restoration." *Waterbirds* 33, no. 2 (June 2010): 193–207. https://manoa.hawaii.edu/hpicesu/papers/2010_changing_seabird_management.pdf.

Gomes, Noah. "Some Traditional Native Hawaiian Bird Hunting Practices on Hawai'i Island." *Hawaiian Journal of History* 50 (2016): 33–51. https://evols.library.manoa.hawaii.edu/server/api /core/bitstreams/1123ba8d-55ec-42bd-a4d2-13cd97ff8a23/content.

Howell, Steve N. G. *Petrels, Albatrosses and Storm-Petrels of North America: A Photographic Guide.* Princeton, NJ: Princeton University Press, 2012.

Howell, Steve N. G., and Kirk Zufelt. *Oceanic Birds of the World: A Photo Guide.* Princeton, NJ: Princeton University Press, 2019.

Lohr, Cheryl A., and Christopher A. Lepczyk. *Desires and Management Preferences of Stakeholders Regarding Feral Cats in the Hawaiian Islands.* Honolulu: Department of Natural Resources and Environmental Management, University of Hawai'i at Mānoa, 2013. https://www.academia. edu/29896705/Desires_and_Management_Preferences_of_Stakeholders _Regarding_Feral_Cats_in_the_Hawaiian_Islands.

Moniz, Jadelyn J. "The Role of Seabirds in Hawaiian Subsistence: Implications for Interpreting Avian Extinction and Extirpation in Polynesia." *Asian Perspectives* 36, no. 1 (Spring 1997). https://scholarspace.manoa.hawaii.edu/items/5c6147bb-0883-4eaa-a376-c70cb0a984b6.

Munro, George C. *Birds of Hawaii.* Rutland, VT: Bridgeway Press/Tuttle, 1960.

Olson, Storrs L., and Helen F. James. "Fossil Birds from the Hawaiian Islands: Evidence for Wholesale Extinction by Man before Western Contact." *Science*, August 13, 1982. https://www.science.org/doi/10.1126/science.217.4560.633.

Ostrom, Peggy H., Anne E. Wiley, Helen F. James, Sam Rossman, William A. Walker, Elise F. Zipkin, and Yoshito Chikaraishi. "Broad-Scale Trophic Shift in the Pelagic North Pacific Revealed by an Oceanic Seabird." *Royal Society Biological Sciences* 284, no. 1851 (March 29, 2017). https://royalsocietypublishing.org/doi/full/10.1098/rspb.2016.2436.

Raine, André F., Scott Driskill, Megan Vynne, Derek Harvey, and Kyle Pias. "Managing the Effects of Introduced Predators on Hawaiian Endangered Seabirds." *Journal of Wildlife Management* 84, no. 3 (January 2020): 425–435. https://wildlife.onlinelibrary.wiley.com/doi/abs/10.1002/ jwmg.21824.

Troy, Jeff R., Nick D. Holmes, Joseph A. Veech, André F. Raine, and M. Clay Green. "Habitat Suitability Modeling for the Endangered Hawaiian Petrel on Kauai and Analysis of Predicted Habitat Overlap with the Newell's Shearwater." *Global Ecology and Conservation* 12 (October 2017): 131–143. https://www.sciencedirect.com/science/article/pii/S2351989417301403?via%3Dihub.

VanZandt, Marie, Donna Delparte, Patrick Hart, Fern Duvall, and Jay Penniman. "Nesting Characteristics and Habitat Use of the Endangered Hawaiian Petrel (Pterodroma sandwichensis) on the Island of Lāna'i." *Waterbirds* 37, no. 1 (March 2014): 43–51. https://www.researchgate.net /publication/260131993_Nesting_Characteristics_and_Habitat_Use_of_the_Endangered _Hawaiian_Petrel_Pterodroma_sandwichensis_on_the_Island_of_Lanai.

Wilson, Scott, and Sheila Buff. *Frohawk's Birds of Hawaii.* Seacausus, NJ: Wellfleet Press, 1989.

Young, L. C., J. H. Behnke, E. A. Vanderwerf, A. F. Raine, C. Mitchell, C. R. Kohley, M. Dalton, M. Mitchell, H. Tonneson, M. DeMotta, G. Wallace, H. Nevins, C. S. Hall, and K. Uyehara. *The Nihoku Ecosystem Restoration Project: A Case Study in Predator Exclusion Fencing, Ecosystem Restoration, and Seabird Translocation.* Pacific Cooperative Studies Unit Technical Report 198. Honolulu: University of Hawai'i at Mānoa, Department of Botany, 2018. http://manoa.hawaii.edu/hpicesu/techr/198/v198.pdf.

ACKNOWLEDGMENTS

Very special thanks to the following people for their support of this book:

To Rachel Sprague, for graciously sharing your work and deep caring for endemic species and ecosystems, and inviting me into the magic of the 'ua'u colony in Lāna'i Hale; to Charlotte Forbes Perry, for opening your beautiful 'ua'u world up to me and including me as a team member for many of your exciting research adventures on Mauna Loa; to Jay Penniman, for sharing Maui and your incredible passion for seabirds, and opening my mind to the conservation possibilities; to Martin Frye and Emily Severson, for energizing me with your love of seabirds and education; to Lindsay Young, Eric VanderWerf, Robby Kohley, Megan Dalton, Erika Dittmar, and Leilani Fowlke, for your inspiring vision and hard work restoring biodiversity and working to create a future for seabirds in Hawai'i; to Cathleen Bailey, for your 'ua'u stories and your powerful connection to place and history, and for reminding me about the importance of remembering; to Ku'ualoha Bailey, for sharing your childhood 'ua'u memories, and helping me find the right name for Makani; to Linda Elliott, for your incredible commitment, vision, and inspiring work; to Rae Okawa and Juan Guerra, for your passionate care of each animal that comes to you for help; to Noah Gomes and Jennifer Waipa, for generously sharing your intimate knowledge and personal history within the culture.

And many thanks to Andre Raine, Fern Duvall, Joy Tamayose, Paul Banko, Alex Wang, Bret Nainoa Mossman, Chris Farmer, and the United States Geological Survey, for the work you do to conserve birds, and for your help with this project. And to Michelle Reynolds and Slater the detection dog, for your tireless work in learning to find seabird burrows and training me to help; to Jess Eden and Jill Lippert, whose hard work and passion are an inspiration to me. And thank you to Andy Collins, Dru Devlin, and Jennifer Stock, for your support.

Sincere thanks to my readers for your valuable feedback: Zack Loebel-Fried, Leayne Patch-Highfill, Harper Highfill, Ryder Barron Brownstein, Kate Werner, Zoey Babcock-Werner, Ilisa Singer, Sally Station, Mary Berman, Raquel Dow, Fia Mattice, Julie Baer, and two anonymous readers who reviewed the manuscript for scientific and cultural accuracy.

Mahalo to University of Hawaiʻi Press for partnering with me to bring important stories of conservation and culture to readers throughout Hawaiʻi and beyond. And many thanks to my cohort there: Emma Ching, Mardee Melton, Carol Abe, and Malia Collins, for helping make this book the best it can be. Many thanks to Rachel Sprague, Peter Pyle, Bret Nainoa Mossman, Archipelago Research and Conservation, and generous eBird contributors. Your excellent photographs and videos of ʻuaʻu helped me bring the birds to life in my art. Much appreciation to Karen Ez for your scanning and color-correcting expertise, and gratitude for my mom: your work still fills me with inspiration!

And thank you always to my husband, for your honest feedback, enthusiastic support of all of my conservation projects, and for sharing this marvelous adventure with me.

In memory of Fern Duvall, whose infectious enthusiasm and dedication to wildlife will live on.

THE TECHNIQUE OF BLOCK PRINTING

The art that appears at the beginning of each chapter in this book is a hand-colored block print. This ancient art form is similar to Hawaiian ʻohe kāpala, bamboo stamping on *kapa*, bark cloth. Caren's process involves carving a recycled rubber block, rolling black ink on the surface, placing paper on the inked surface, and then pulling her print. Once it's dry, she colors the print with watercolor pencils.

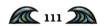

ABOUT THE AUTHOR

Photo courtesy of Neil Fried.

Caren Keʻalaokapualehua Loebel-Fried is an award-winning author and artist from Volcano, Hawaiʻi. Birds, conservation, and the natural world are the foundations of her work. Caren has created eight storybooks to date, including *Manu, the Boy Who Loved Birds* (2020), *Hawaiian Legends of the Guardian Spirits* (2002), *A Perfect Day for an Albatross* (2017), *Legend of the Gourd* (2010), and *Lono and the Magical Land beneath the Sea* (2006). Her books have received multiple awards, including from the American Folklore Society, Moonbeam Children's Book Awards, and the Hawaiʻi Book Publishers Association. Caren has produced educational art for many organizations and agencies including the U.S. Fish and Wildlife Service, Midway Atoll National Wildlife Refuge, Kīlauea Point Natural History Association, Conservation Council for Hawaiʻi, and Friends of Hanauma Bay. Caren created the art in this book with hand-colored, hand-pulled block prints and pencil drawings. She learned the art of block printing from her mother.

Caren's love of seabirds is fueled by fieldwork on Midway Atoll with the albatross census team and research of the ʻuaʻu, the Hawaiian petrel, and other seabirds on their breeding grounds throughout the Hawaiian Islands. She aims to bring people closer to the natural world in the hope that they will want to help care for it.